Max
Spaniel

FUNNY

LUNCH

David Catrow

Orchard Books
An Imprint of Scholastic Inc.
New York

For Bubbs, who tells me all his stories — D.C.

Text and illustrations copyright © 2010 by David Catrow

All rights reserved. Published by Orchard Books, an imprint of Scholastic Inc.,
Publishers since 1920. ORCHARD BOOKS and design are registered trademarks of Watts
Publishing Group, Ltd., used under license. SCHOLASTIC and associated logos are
trademarks and/or registered trademarks of Scholastic Inc.

Library of Congress Cataloging-in-Publication Data is available.
ISBN 978-0-545-05747-9
10 9 8 7 6 5 4 3 2 1   10 11 12 13 14
Printed in Singapore 46
Reinforced Binding for Library Use
First edition, May 2010

The artwork was created using watercolors.
The display text was set in Good Girl.
The series display text was set in Mandingo.
The text was set in Old Style 1.
Book design by Whitney Lyle

My name is Max.
I am not a dog.

I am a great chef.

AX SPANIEL

My great-great-great-great-
great-great-great-great-great-
great-great-great-great-great-
grandpa Ax Spaniel was a chef.

When I get dressed,
I have to look
just right.

No.

No.

No.

YES!

We wash our paws before we work.

We make the special of the day – pizza pie.

We roll.
We pat.

We toss.

We put the pizza pie in the oven.

Lunch is busy.

A tummy growls. I growl back.

Everyone is hungry.

"Welcome to Max's.
Would you like to try the special?"

"No, thank you," he says. "Chili for me!"

So, I bring him a scarf.

"This will warm you up."

"Welcome to Max's.
Would you like to try the special?"

"No, thank you," she replies.
"I will have a hot dog."

So, I bring her a hot dog.

I sing.

I dance.

I do a little magic.

I hear the take-out bell.

The driver barks,
"One hundred pizzas
     with everything."

Yippee!

We mix.

We roll.

We bake.

Oh no! It is not a pizza pie. It is a pizza mess. What are we going to do?

A great chef thinks on his feet.

We race to Joe's Pizza Palace.

We race back with

a leaning tower of pizzas!

Pizzas for everyone.

A pizza party for us!

DAVID CATROW

is the creator of the
Max spaniel series.
Dinosaur Hunt is the
first book and *Funny
Lunch* is the second
book. Max spaniel is based upon
David's dog Bubbs.

David Catrow lives with
his wife, Debbie, and their
dogs in springfield, Ohio.

You can visit David at
www.catrow.com.